The Monster Of The Woods!

For my friend Nancy
~ CF
Per Arianna, ti amo sempre di più
~ RJ

Text copyright © 2009 by Claire Freedman
Illustrations copyright © 2009 by Russell Julian
First published in Great Britain in 2009 by Scholastic
Children's Books as *Tappity-Tap! What Was That?*

ISBN 978-0-545-56837-1

Library of Congress Cataloging-in-Publication
Data available

10 9 8 7 6 5 4 3 2 1   13 14 15 16 17

Printed in Singapore   46
First Scholastic U.S. edition, September 2013

The Monster Of The Woods!

by Claire Freedman
& Russell Julian

CARTWHEEL BOOKS
An Imprint of Scholastic Inc.

Deep in the woods, Owl, Mouse, and Rabbit
were having a **Very Important Meeting**.

VERY
IMPORTANT
MEETING

"This is a Very Important Meeting,"
said Owl. "We need to do something about
the Monster Of The Woods."
"I'm scared!" cried Rabbit.
"No one's safe while It's around!" squeaked Mouse.

"I've heard he's **very big** and **horribly hairy!**" Mouse gulped.
"And very, very **scary**." Rabbit trembled.

"Don't panic!" said Owl, handing around notes
he had written out neatly for everyone.
"I'm sure we have nothing to worry about.
But just in case, I have a plan."

"Remember," said Owl, "the Monster Of The Woods probably won't come calling at all."

"He will if it's dark and stormy enough." Rabbit shivered.

"And if he's hungry enough!" added Mouse.

"Don't worry," said Owl. "As long as we follow my plan, we'll be safe."

That night, it was dark, and it was stormy.
Owl woke up with a start.

CRASH! BANG! CRASH!

"It's only the thunder," he thought.

HOWL! HOWL! HOWL!

"It's only the wind,"
he told himself.

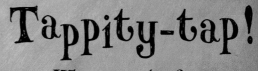

Tappity-tap!

What was that?

Quick as he could, Owl locked the door,
pulled the curtains shut,
and pretended he was not at home.

"Let me in, Owl," called Rabbit.
"I thought I heard the
Monster Of The Woods.
And I'm getting drenched!"

"Come in, Rabbit,"
said Owl. "It's only a
nasty, noisy storm."

Rabbit scurried inside.

Tappity-tap!

What was that?

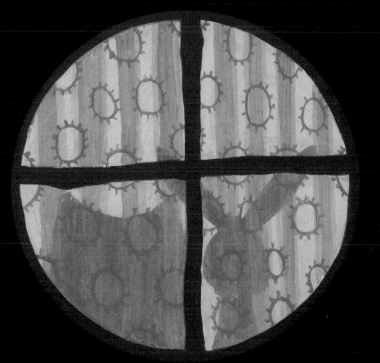

"Quick!" cried Owl. "The plan!"

So they locked the door,
pulled the curtains shut,
and pretended they were not at home.

"Come in, Mouse," said Owl.
"It's only a noisy, nasty storm."
Mouse curled up by the fire.

"Let me in, Owl," called Mouse.
"I thought I heard the
Monster Of The Woods.
And I'm freezing!"

Owl made some nice hot cocoa.
"See?" he said. "We're all safe now."

Tappity-tap-TAP!

What was that?

Rabbit dropped his mug in fright.

"Is that Mouse knocking on the front door?" he whispered.

"I'm already here, silly," Mouse squeaked.

"Is it Owl, then?" Rabbit gulped.

"I'm here, too!" Owl cried.

The friends looked at each other.

"Oh no," they all whispered together. "It must be . . .

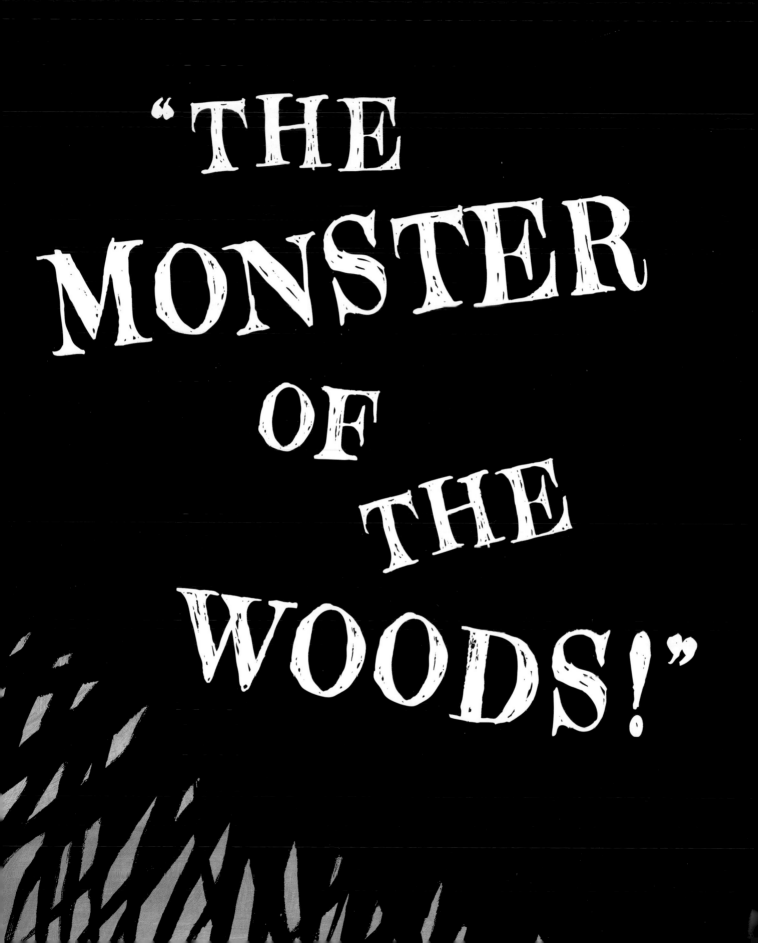

"Stay calm," shouted Owl. "Remember my plan!"

So they locked the door,
pulled the curtains shut,
and pretended they were not at home.

THUMP! THUMP! THUMP!

The banging got

louder and louder...

"Sniffle... snuffle... SQUEAK!"

"That noise doesn't sound like a monster."
Rabbit frowned, forgetting to pretend
they were not at home.

"It sounds like crying," said Mouse,
nervously opening the curtains.
"Whoever it is sounds frightened,"
agreed Owl. "Maybe they need help."
He peeked through the peephole...

Slowly, Owl unlocked the door.
A tiny, bedraggled, furry thing stood on the doorstep.

"Who are YOU?" everyone gasped.

"I'm the Monster Of The Woods!"

"You?" said Mouse. "You're not very big!"

"I'm bigger than you," It said.

"You're not horribly hairy, either!" added Rabbit.

"I flatten in the rain," It replied.

"And you're not at all scary," said Owl.

"It's true," the Monster sighed. "I don't know why everyone is so frightened of me!"

CRASH! BANG! CRASH!

The Monster leapt into Owl's arms.
"I hate thunder!" he whimpered.
"There, there." Owl patted him kindly.
"We're all safe now."

It was the next **Very Important Meeting.**
Owl handed around notes he had written
out neatly for everyone.
"Before we begin," Owl beamed,
"let's welcome. . .

"the Monster Of The Woods!"
The Monster giggled,
    "But my friends call me Snuggles!"
    And everyone agreed,
Snuggles was the perfect name!

WHaT TO DO IF
YOU aRE STUCK UP
a Tall TREE :

1. MaKE a COMFY SEat
    OUT OF LEaVES.

2. WaVE a LOT.

3. SHOUT FOR HELP.

P.S. NEXT WEEK BRING
PaPER aND STRING.
WE SHALL BE
MaKING
OUR OWN
PaRaCHUTES.

The End